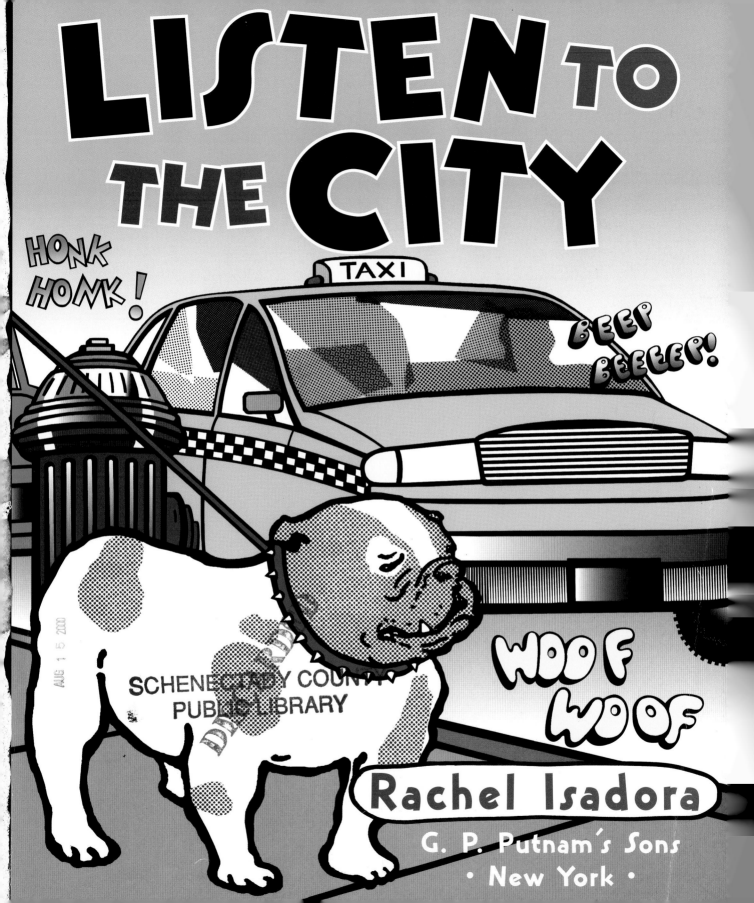

Copyright © 2000 by Rachel Isadora
All rights reserved. This book, or parts thereof, may not be reproduced in any form
without permission in writing from the publisher.
G. P. Putnam's Sons, a division of Penguin Putnam Books for Young Readers,
345 Hudson Street, New York, NY 10014.
G. P. Putnam's Sons, Reg. U.S. Pat. & Tm. Off. Published simultaneously in Canada.
Printed in Hong Kong by South China Printing Co. (1988) Ltd. Book designed by Semadar Megged.
Text set in CircusMouseBook-Medium.
Library of Congress Cataloging-in-Publication Data
Isadora, Rachel. Listen to the city / by Rachel Isadora. p. cm. Summary: Illustrations and
simple text describe the sights and sounds of a day in the city. [1. City and town life—Fiction.
2. Sound—Fiction.] I. Title. PZ7.1763Lm 1999 [E]—DC21 98-20282 CIP AC
ISBN 0-399-23047-5
1 3 5 7 9 10 8 6 4 2
First Impression

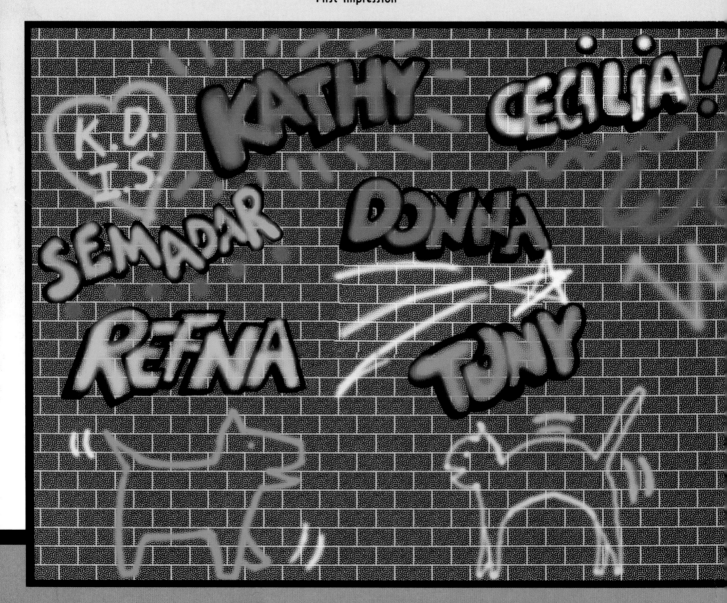

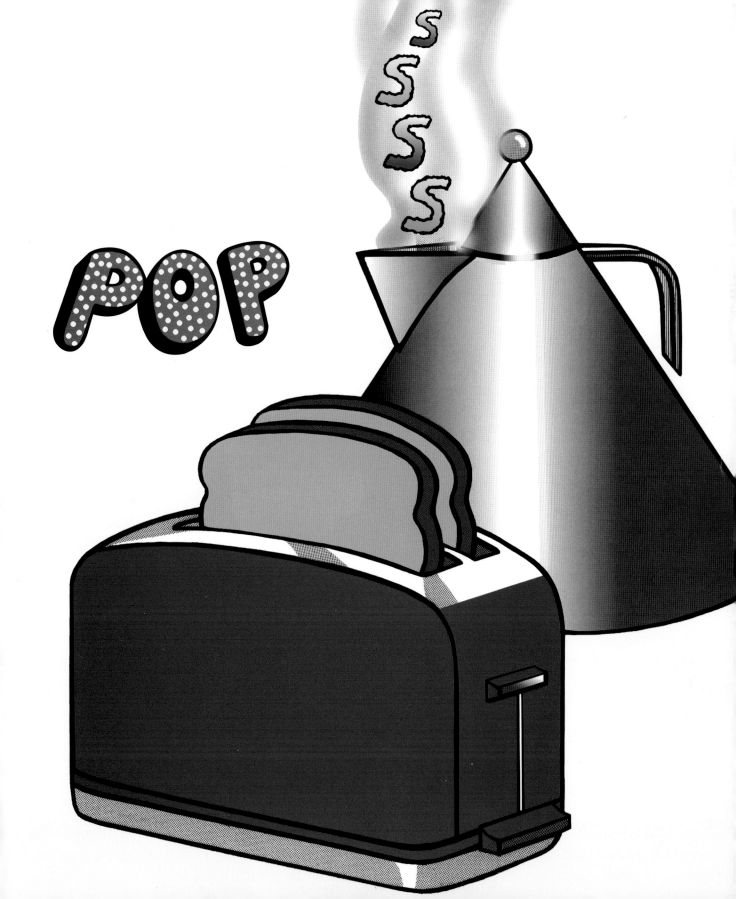